Nothing To See Here
K'Barthan Extras, Hamgeean Misfit: No 2

Nothing To See Here

K'Barthan Extras, Hamgeean Misfit: No 2

by

M T McGuire

Hamgee University Press

First published February 2020 by
Hamgee University Press

ISBN-978-1-907809-32-3

Nothing To See Here is written in British English with a couple of instances of light swearing. Estimated UK film rating of this book : PG (Parental Guidance).

Written by M T McGuire
Edited by Emma Wilkins
Published by Hamgee University Press
Cover design by A Trouble Halved

M T McGuire is over 50 years old now but still checks inside
unfamiliar wardrobes for a gateway to Narnia.
Boringly, she's not found any.

Thank you for buying this book.
If you enjoyed it you can keep up with
news of the author online by
visiting www.hamgee.co.uk

You can also sign up for the
M T McGuire mailing list by visiting
http://www.hamgee.co.uk/freebook
and even buy K'Barthan Series merchandise at
http://bit.ly/UHSUshop

Chapter 1
Another job

The Pan of Hamgee sat quietly at a corner table in the Parrot and Screwdriver pub on Turnadot Street. As usual Humbert, the eponymous parrot who went with the Screwdriver, had recognised a soft touch and made a beeline for him.

'Wipe my conkers!' Humbert shouted, circling The Pan's head excitedly.

'Here you go.'

The Pan was a dab hand at this now. He'd bought a packet of crisps, which he opened and spread on the empty table next to his, to act as a parrot decoy. Humbert landed on the back of a nearby chair and hopped onto the table, clawing and pecking happily at them. On one level The Pan congratulated himself that Humbert had fallen for his plan. On another, he felt a grudging admiration for any creature that could inveigle a packet of crisps out of him with such ease every time he came into the pub.

Winter was deepening, the shortest day was coming up soon and the weather was cold and damp, a horrible combination. The Pan had been sleeping in his wheels for some weeks now. When he couldn't, those times when the they were at the repair shop, for example, he kept walking through the night, and found somewhere warm and unobtrusive to sleep during the day. In this bitter weather that was the only way. To sleep outside at night was a sure way to die of hypothermia.

It was just over a month since The Pan had become a messenger for Big Merv, and true to his word, the Big Thing was paying a small retainer each week. It wasn't enough to pay rent on a room or even to live on, but it did cover important things like trips to the bath house or the launderette, both of which were important for a man who needs to blend in unobtrusively, or, from time to time, hide. After all, there was no point in being good at running away from people if they could smell your presence. Big Merv had paid extra for both the delivery jobs The Pan had undertaken too. In return, The Pan had been very careful to make sure that, where his lack of means required him to steal some essential, he didn't nick it from anywhere on Big Merv's patch. With the Big Thing's help, The Pan was definitely keeping … well, to say he was keeping out of trouble was an overstatement, but there were some days when nobody chased him. Even better, he'd not had a delivery to make in over a week. While the extra cash from deliveries always came in handy, the danger that went with each job held less appeal. Yeh. He smiled to himself as he looked into his pint. All was quiet and that was good.

"S a letter arrived,' said Gladys, dumping it unceremoniously on the table in front of him.

Or maybe not.

'Thank you,' The Pan sighed as she retired back to the Holy of Holies, behind the bar. Over the burble of conversation among the punters, he could hear her cutting slices of bread. Clearly someone had ordered sandwiches.

He turned his attention back to the envelope and looked at the handwriting. It was Big Merv's. It would be, wouldn't it? *That'll teach me to get smug*, he thought.

Two whole weeks of quiet was probably a bit much to expect. The previous one was gift enough.

Right then, another job, another brush with death, or at least it would be if the last one was anything to go on. Not that he was complaining too much. As a Government Blacklisted Individual—a GBI—his whole life was a brush with death anyway, so it hardly made much difference. Putting aside the authorities' efforts to find him and kill him, The Pan had little more confidence in his new boss. Working for Big Merv didn't so much feel like earning a living as securing a longer reprieve from impending murder with each success. Big Merv seemed fair, The Pan had to give him that, but he was also scary, intensely so. And while he did listen, he didn't brook fools gladly. That was enough to put The Pan on defensive alert because he had to admit it to himself, he was a bit of a pillock sometimes, and he asked a lot of questions.

He read the letter. *'Delivery: collect a box from Mrs Dingleton's bakery on Frontock Street by three thirty pm.'*

That figured. Big Merv was a Thing who respected quality and Mrs Dingleton's bakery was the best in town. He read on. *'Deliver to Arnhelm Gaspot and colleagues in time for tea at the Garden View Hotel on Waterfront Road at four pm, The Ghengis suite. Report to The Big Thing nightclub—staff door—at four thirty pm.'*

The Pan knew exactly what the contents of this package were. Pastries. Today was a day when K'Barthans traditionally exchanged pastries. It was the eve of Arnold, The Prophet's Birthday, a fact that had once been the cause of considerable celebration in K'Barth, until the Grongles banned all religious activity.

Arnold of Nim, or The Graciously Exalted Prophet, Arnold of Nim (to give him his full title) was the first spiritual and temporal ruler of K'Barth and founding father of the nation's only religion, Nimmism.

Nimmism was pretty straightforward. It centred round one commandment, that all beings should be decent to one another. There was a wealth of theological guidance as to how this was done, of course, in the form of eight books of sayings of The Prophet and another seven about how to be decent to one another, but that was all optional stuff.

As well as this very simple premise, Nimmism came with a lot of spectacular festivals—Arnold, The Prophet's Birthday being one of them. There were few things the average K'Barthan liked more than an excuse for a really good party and the Nimmist faith gave them lots. Pretty much everyone in K'Barth was a Nimmist in one form or another, although obviously (since the Grongles made it illegal) not officially.

The Pan had never quite grasped why the Grongles had banned religion. Something about it being detrimental to society. But it was difficult to see how being decent to one another would be detrimental, except when people got it wrong and became so ardent about one particular aspect or another of Arnold's teachings they forgot that being kind to one another was the actual point. But that was just *people* being detrimental to society, wasn't it? Not religion.

Perhaps being decent to one another was detrimental to Grongolian society, The Pan mused, since they really didn't seem to be able to get the hang of it. Or perhaps they were decent to each other, and it was being decent to K'Barthans they were struggling with. Whatever the reason for the ban, it didn't really make much difference. It was still perfectly possible to be an ardent Nimmist and to go about being decent to others without the authorities noticing. You just couldn't go to the temple once a week anymore.

Arnold's Birthday and Arnold's Birthday Eve used to be big events in K'Barth; national holiday, fire crackers in the streets and a huge meal made up of a variety of traditional and regional foods and alcoholic beverages, none of which went with the other, and the giving of pastries.

It appeared that, gang lord or not, Big Merv was still a devout enough Nimmist to send Prophet's Birthday Pastries to his friends and associates, and he wanted The Pan to deliver some.

'Well, well, well,' said The Pan as he folded the letter up and put it in his pocket.

'Good news?' asked Gladys, who'd delivered the sandwiches to the madam from the brothel opposite, Betsy Coed, along with a couple of her girls who were having the night off, and was now collecting some empty glasses from a nearby table.

The Pan shrugged. 'Sort of.'

'Work?'

'Sort of.'

'My, you is enigmatic,' Gladys said drily.

'Mmm.' The Pan raised an eyebrow at her. 'That's me.'

He glanced at his watch. One o'clock. He knew the hotel, and he was pretty sure the Ghengis suite was on the first floor at the front. He'd take a quick walk up there to double check, then he could head back to Mrs Dingleton's nice and early so he could be sure to leave by three thirty.

'Is you in tonight?' Gladys broke into this thoughts.

'Mmm?' He looked up at her and she gave him one of the most theatrical winks he'd ever seen anyone do. 'Why?' he asked. 'You're not—'

'Not Celebrating The Prophet's Birthday?' said Gladys, definitely giving it all capitals. 'Ner, we isn't.'

That hadn't been The Pan's original question. He'd merely been going to ask if they were up to something, but he let it ride.

Ada who had clearly been listening to their conversation, made her way over to them. 'We would never do anything that breaks the law, would we Gladys?'

'Ner.'

'So you're Not Celebrating Arnold, The Prophet's Birthday here tonight?' The Pan said.

'That's right, we're not,' said Ada whistling nonchalantly. One of the punters—it sounded like Fred 'Fingers' Davies but The Pan couldn't be sure—snickered quietly into their beer. 'It's not The Prophet's Birthday tonight, after all, the actual *day* is tomorrow. What we are having tonight is merely a celebratory meal.'

''S right. Can't be celebrating Arnold's Birthday tonight can we? On account of that it isn't Arnold's Birthday.'

'I see,' said The Pan. He raised his eyebrow at the old ladies again. 'So what *are* you celebrating?'

'Nothing,' said Ada.

''S right,' agreed Gladys.

'Ah right, I see.' The Pan replied.

'Yer. BUT we has happened upon the ingredients for the traditional meal, see. Completely coincidentally, mind—'

'Exactly, and it would be criminal to waste it, wouldn't it, Gladys?'

'Yer. 'S quail with hot herbs—'

'Isn't that splendid!' Ada clapped her hands and bobbed up and down. 'We can even do that curried squid dish—'

'The one they does in Hamgee, which we isn't going ter do unless there's someone here who can eat it.'

Celebrating The Prophet's Birthday might have been banned, but clearly that wasn't going to stop Gladys, Ada, Their Trev and the punters at the Parrot and Screwdriver from Not Celebrating his birthday very thoroughly.

'Arnold!' said The Pan in pretend horror. 'Curried squid!'

'Don't blaspheme, dear,' chided Ada.

'Sorry, but look … if you need someone to help you eat those terrible things, I'd be happy to assist.'

'Yer, thought you might. I has seen how you puts away my chutney.'

'So you think you can make it,' Ada paused delicately, 'after work?'

He could almost hear the air quotes either side of the word 'work' as she said it.

'I should be able to. It depends how "work" goes,' said The Pan.

'Humph,' said Gladys.

'What time should I arrive for this party you're not having?'

'We're starting service at six pm tonight,' said Ada.

"Cept we isn't,' said Gladys putting her finger on the side of her nose and making another ridiculously theatrical wink.

'Then I must be sure I'm here to see it Not Happen,' said The Pan with a smile.

Chapter 2
The pick up

Mrs Dingleton was a member of what was known in K'Barth as 'the smaller furry genera'. In this case, a Spiffle. That meant she was about three feet tall and covered in orange fur. She had a face a little like a large rodent; pointy inquisitive nose, black button eyes, whiskers and rounded ears. Spiffles often ended up being chefs in K'Barth. The Pan suspected it was as much to do with their reputation for being personable and good with other beings as their cookery skills. Yeh, it probably took good management skills to run a kitchen. That said, a lot of Spiffles *were* excellent cooks. They seemed to be able to combine the spicy hotness of K'Barth's regional cuisine with the aggressively bland neutrality of the food traditional to Ning Dang Po in a manner that pleased all parties.

Mrs Dingleton's bakery was staffed mostly—exclusively today it seemed—by Spiffles like herself. The place was bustling with activity when The Pan arrived, just before three. He was glad he'd decided to go there early. Despite the identity of his boss, or maybe because of it, he was treated as merely one of several people waiting to pick up pastries. That said, there were no actual Prophet's Birthday pastries in evidence. The glass-fronted display under the counter was stocked with the usual fare: cream horns, custard tarts, fruit flans, brandy snaps and other delicacies. Although, as it was nearing the end of her working day, Mrs Dingleton had few of those left. Mostly, the display cases held empty frilly doilies where the cakes and pastries had *been.* Likewise, the shelves behind the counter, which were usually groaning with harvest loaves, tall loaves, fat loaves, wholemeal loaves and a whole host of other dough-based delicacies ranged in rows, were empty too.

Due to the fact that Spiffles like Mrs Dingleton are small, the shelves were equipped with a series of platforms on pulleys. These were used to reach the loftiest delicacies by the many assistants of her own genus that Mrs Dingleton employed. Sometimes, an assistant would be stationed up there for the duration, throwing loaves down to their colleagues below as and when they were requested. It was a sight to see when the shop was busy. One of the assistants was up there now with a pail of water, cleaning the uppermost surfaces with a scrubbing brush and then drying them with a cloth. The Pan didn't dare do more than glance through the window much of the time. He was rather scruffier than Mrs Dingleton's usual kind of customer and feared he would stand out, or be recognised as a GBI by the wrong type of customer.

As Ning Dang Po's premier baker, Mrs Dingleton could get rationed ingredients where others couldn't. This was partly because more than a couple of Grongles were partial to her work these days and they ensured their source of favourite pastries was well supplied, as it was only K'Barthans for whom these things were in short order. It also helped that her K'Barthan customer base included many people like Big Merv, who had the same love of consistency in supply, along with the kind of 'contacts' who would also procure contraband or rationed ingredients if she needed them.

However, Mrs Dingleton still husbanded her supplies carefully. She abhorred waste and learned the whims and delights of her customers so well that she seldom had more than a handful of cakes left at the end of each day. These she gave away. K'Barthans of dubious status, like The Pan, would wait for her at a disused warehouse on Canal Quay where she went with her leftovers, ostensibly to feed them to the ducks but usually to feed the poor, the weary and in The Pan's case, outlaws who the government had blacklisted.

Even though closing time wasn't until four, the late rush had already started. Business was being done on two levels, of course—above and below the counter. The Prophet's Birthday pastries weren't officially on sale, even though The Pan, and others, knew they were. As a result many customers were buying a single pastry for a very inflated price. Strangely, they all seemed to want their pastries wrapped, as well. In each instance the pastry would be carefully removed from the display case with tongs and whisked off through the doorway behind the counter. The Pan, along with the other customers, would then catch a tantalising glimpse into the bakery proper, through the blue, white and yellow plastic strips hanging there to stop flies and prying eyes. Somewhere in its hallowed depths, the assistant would 'wrap' the pastry and return with a very oversized box because 'the small boxes we ordered didn't come this morning'. The Pan watched as this happened again and again. It was clear, as each customer grabbed their prize, that the box was far too heavy to contain just the one pastry.

Needless to say, the shop ran a strict policy of first-come, first-served and The Pan was very much last-come. He watched as the two Spiffles behind the counter set about serving everyone else. Well, he'd left himself plenty of extra time so it shouldn't matter. Once he'd made the assistant aware of his presence and failed to secure any leeway for being there at Big Merv's behest, The Pan sat on the windowsill and watched the world go by outside the shop, while listening to the soft drone of the conversations within it. Everyone was fed up with the cold weather, and most were worried about money, but they were putting their fears aside for the moment while they Took No Part in the banned festivities to celebrate The Prophet's Birthday which were Not Happening, at all, anywhere. It was warm and dry in the shop and nobody in the throng of people pressed around the counter seemed bothered by The Pan while, to his delight, none of the Grongolian security forces members walking past outside seemed bothered either.

The Pan leaned back against the window. Before long the warm atmosphere of the shop got to him and he began to doze. By the time the crowd thinned as people went home with their single overpriced item in its oversized box, stuffed to the gunwales with contraband Prophet's Birthday Pastries, The Pan was asleep. He was woken by a voice.

'Young gentleman, I believe this one is for you!' it said.

He hurriedly jumped to his feet. Arnold's snot! How long had it been? The other customers had all left and the shop was empty. He made to look at his watch.

'It's twenty to four,' said the voice.

Arnold's trollies! thought The Pan. 'Thanks,' he said.

As he stepped up to the counter, he found Mrs Dingleton herself holding a large box which was fastened closed with a red ribbon. She was wearing an apron and, true to every stereotype about the preferences of Spiffles as a species, one of the most impressively ornate hats The Pan had ever seen. He found himself putting his own hat on having taken it off earlier. He'd heard that this was a way of showing hat respect, which is important to Spiffles. It was certainly important to Mrs Dingleton by the looks of things.

Essentially, Mrs Dingleton's hat was one of those white trilbies catering folk wear, except it was oh so much more than that. It was adorned with doughnuts, pastries and other finery crafted in felt with a peacock feather that bobbed and wobbled every time she moved. Alongside the box, she held a notebook. She disappeared from sight for a moment as the counter hid her from view and then suddenly her face was at The Pan's eye level as she hopped onto a high stool. From the stool, she stepped onto the counter top, itself. The hat was even more distracting close up.

'Good afternoon,' said The Pan politely.

She consulted the notebook. '"Young man, hat, shifty,"' she read. 'Yes, I think you fit that description,' she put the notebook down and looked at him more closely. 'Don't I see you down at the quay from time to time?' she asked. Before The Pan could confirm that, she continued. 'This box is yours, let me just …' she leaned over the counter a bit to look at him more closely, 'yes, dark blue eyes, definitely, this one's for you.' A beat. 'One of my finest four-portion pastries, if I do say so myself. Of course, a larger one like this allows me more room to work. There is so much more scope for detailing on the face.'

'I'm sure the recipient will be very grateful,' said The Pan as he took the package from her.

'Better than that other group of fools then,' she said.

'I'm sorry?'

'Some swine ordered pastries for fifty and hasn't collected them.'

'He might.'

'Huh! Some hope,' she said. 'If the rumour mill is correct—and it usually is—he was arrested for breaking and entering last night. I doubt we'll see him around for some time. Serves him right for working in the run-up to a holy holiday,' she complained, clearly turning a spectacularly myopic eye to her own activities. 'Even so, fancy doing that to himself,' she tutted. 'He was one of my best customers and now I'm stuck with his illegal pastries. Do you know anyone who'd want fifty Arnold's Birthday mini-pastries at short notice?' she demanded.

'I might …' The Pan thought of Gladys and Ada and how delighted they would be if he turned up to Not Celebrate Arnold's Birthday at the Parrot and Screwdriver with fifty pastries from Mrs Dingleton. 'I'm not in a position to pay for them though, unfortunately.' No, hang on, Big Merv would pay The Pan something when he reported back at The Big Thing. 'At least, not much and not at the moment,' The Pan added. 'But if you could wait until I—'

'Oh, I don't need paying much, I just can't bear throwing them away.'

'Really?' asked The Pan in surprise.

'Of course, just a token amount, five K'Barthan Zloty will do.'

Five Zloty? Was she serious? Even The Pan would be able to afford five Zloty or at least, he would when he was paid for the delivery he was about to make. No surely this was too good to be true, he'd misunderstood or something.

'Are you sure you couldn't sell them tomorrow,' said The Pan, just to check.

Judging by her reaction, the casual observer could have been forgiven for thinking he had just asked Mrs Dingleton to roast one of her children alive over a slow fire.

'I have standards of freshness,' she said, folding her arms.

'Well, in that case, I know some people who'd be happy to eat them for you. I'm here to collect, though, and I won't have the cash to pay for them until I've delivered this one,' The Pan explained. 'If you can keep them for me, I should be able to pop by later.'

Her beady black eyes narrowed. 'Are you certain you can't take them now?'

He rummaged in his pocket and pressed the button on his keys that would summon his vehicle.

'I can, but only if you're happy to take an IOU.'

Mrs Dingleton's eyes narrowed a little more. The Pan

suspected that was a 'no'. Not surprising really. He knew he wouldn't have accepted an IOU from someone like him.

'Can I come back for them? If it's not too inconvenient, I mean?'

'When?'

How long would it take to deliver the pastry to Big Merv's contacts at the Garden View Hotel, report to Big Merv's nightclub and collect payment, The Pan wondered. Not too long, surely. It depended if the security forces took an interest, he supposed.

'In an hour maybe, or an hour and a quarter, I *will* come back, I promise.'

She took a long slow breath in and then made a kind of tutting, whistling noise as she let it out again. Clearly she was thinking the matter over. 'I was hoping to shut the shop by four … I tell you what, I've a little more stock to sell, I will stay open until five but no later.'

'Done,' said The Pan. 'Thank you, you're a marvel.'

They shook hands on it and she gave him the box he was to deliver for Big Merv.

He left the shop and the bell tinkled as he closed the door behind him. The snurd was already waiting for him, parked beside the pavement with the engine running and the roof folded back ready for him to jump in. He checked his watch; ten to four. He'd never make it to the Garden View Hotel on foot and was glad he'd summoned wheels. Like any K'Barthan who owned a vehicle, The Pan drove a snurd, made by the Great Snurd (of K'Barth) Company Limited. This model was called an SE2, but far away in another version of reality it looked like a late 1960s/early 1970s Lotus Elan.

Clearly, The Pan's wheels were like their owner and entered on a police database somewhere. However, unlike their interest in The Pan, the authorities' interest in the SE2 seemed sporadic (or perhaps their use of the database in question was less routine). There were times though, when being pursued was fairly inevitable—and this was one of those times. Ideally, The Pan would have preferred to walk because, at the moment, it involved less hassle. Unfortunately, being late delivering Big Merv's Not The Prophet's Birthday Pastry to Arnhelm Gaspot—whoever he was—and friends at the Garden View Hotel wasn't an option.

Yeh.

'Needs must,' muttered The Pan as he opened the passenger door and placed the cake box carefully on the seat. 'Life is all about choices,' he added, quoting one of the Sayings of The Prophet as he carefully secured it with the seat belt. The odds of survival were better if he was being chased by some bunch of Grongolian numpties than if he annoyed his boss. He shut the door carefully, leapt over the bonnet and vaulted into the driver's seat without opening the door, like a boy racer. Uh-oh. Shouldn't have done that. It was the wave of disapproval he felt first, before he even saw the three Grongles in security forces uniforms across the street. They always operated in threes. Apparently this was because one might go their own way and two could always conspire. But if there were three, and they planned anything untoward, one would always inform. As The Pan looked straight at them, the nearest pointed something towards him. It looked like a static-powered, hand-held personal computer—oh no, wait, he was an officer, so it was an army issue smart-phone. He'd be using the face recognition software.

'Arnold's bum! That's all I need,' The Pan muttered, turning his head swiftly away from them. He wasn't sure if he'd faced them long enough for the phone to get a match but if his experience had taught him anything it was to be cautious. Yes, it was probably best to assume it had. He wasn't sure how the face recognition software worked because, as a K'Barthan, he wasn't allowed a personal computer or a mobile phone, let alone access to an app. From his previous experience on the receiving end, though, it usually took ten or fifteen seconds for the software to produce a result. Rumour was it was only accurate up to about thirty feet.

Perhaps he should ask Big Merv about it. The Big Thing, as he was often called, had a mobile phone himself (and a personal computer) so he might know more. The Pan wasn't sure who his boss called on it—other gang lords presumably. Because of the law against K'Barthans owning a mobile, it was doubtful many of Big Merv's contacts would have one. As The Pan swiftly fastened his seatbelt, he recalled the sumptuous house he'd visited up in The Planes for his first delivery job. The lady Swamp Thing living there, Ms Myrtle, she probably did. Perhaps Big Merv called her, thought The Pan as he swiped the fingerprint reader on the dash.

'Fingerprint ident checked; perfect match,' said the voice of his snurd. A female voice which The Pan considered to be very sexy.

'Thank you,' he said before he could stop himself. Talking to a machine? He was going mental. He wondered about using aviator mode and flying there. The sticky wing was unfolding better now that Gerry had worked on it. Really, it needed a part as he still had to lean out and hit it with a hammer sometimes, but not always. Probably best not to fly in front of the Grongles. 'Natives' using aviator was frowned upon.

'Right then.' He pressed the button to close the roof and risked another glance at the Grongles across the road. They were all looking at the phone, presumably reading the results, except they seemed to be unsure. How far away was he then, he wondered. More than thirty feet? Possibly. Was it far enough? Who knew? One of the Grongles looked up suddenly and saw The Pan watching.

'Go time. Hands at quarter to three, mirror, signal, manoeuvre. We're not in a hurry, just cruising, we're not in a hurry, just cruising … until we're out of their sight,' he muttered to himself as he drove carefully into the traffic.

He checked behind him. One of the joys of having eyes in the back of his head was that he didn't actually need to use the mirror, except when he was trying to convince traffic police that he was driving with due care and attention, of course. Then he had to make sure they saw his head moving at regular intervals. The Grongles had summoned two police snurds which were just arriving beside them.

'Smecking marvellous,' muttered The Pan as, still driving in what he called 'granny mode', he turned the corner out of their sight. Good. Now he could get a move on.

Chapter 3
Disaster

The Pan of Hamgee floored the accelerator, nipped down a side road and pressed the button on the dash marked 'Aviator'. As the wings unfurled, he accelerated sharply and took off. Climbing above the houses, he saw the two Grongle patrol vehicles flash past the bottom of the road at speed. Had he lost them that easily? He could hope, but as he rose above the buildings, the Grongle vehicles appeared again, this time rising skyward from the main road, also in aviator mode.

Ah. Not good.

There was a wailing sound as the patrol vehicles put their sirens on.

'Mmm, full blues and twos,' muttered The Pan. The recognition software must have worked. He glanced at his watch as he accelerated. 'Ten minutes.'

The hotel was only a short flip by air but The Pan was horribly aware that he would be hard put to lose two patrol cars and make Big Merv's delivery at the exact time he was supposed to. He was gladder than ever now that he'd walked up there and looked it over first.

The two snurds were coming up fast, but so far, they didn't appear to have called for back-up. That figured. There was a decent price on The Pan's head these days. For his pursuers, that seemed to have made it less about the thrill of the chase and more about the prospect of a reward. The bigger the reward became, the longer they took to call for back-up, presumably because they wanted it all for themselves. The Pan thanked The Prophet for their greed and, with a quick glance at the pastries on the seat beside him, accelerated.

A bolt of laser fire flew past him. *Uh-oh, straight in with the hard stuff.* Perhaps he should have stopped and played innocent?

No.

Then again, acrobatics were right out unless he could drive one-handed and hold the box steady with the other.

No, he'd never be able to do that. And even if he could, the pastry might still be damaged. He couldn't risk that. OK so he could probably get away with a small corner broken off here and there but if he ruined it, and Big Merv found out, he was a dead man. Then again, putting aside that, as a blacklisted being, his existence was treason, The Pan knew the Grongles took a dim view of pastry possession. Yeh. If they stopped him and found a four portion pastry from Mrs Dingleton's about his person, it would probably make him a dead man on two counts.

One of the security forces officers was shouting at him through a megaphone, but he was concentrating on driving and didn't pay much attention to what they were saying.

He'd just have to outrun them and try not to damage his cargo. He took another quick glance at his watch.

Unless he could find a way to be smart about this. He needed to get the jump on them, but without recourse to anything that might shake the pastry about any more than necessary.

He slowed up and listened. Ah yes, now he could make out what they were shouting at him. They wanted him to land. Waterfront Road wasn't far but he'd never get into the hotel with this lot on his tail.

'Only one thing for it,' he sighed, eased his foot off the accelerator and let the SE2 lose a bit more speed.

He had a plan. It was rubbish but it would probably get

the pastry to Big Merv's friends on time and with any luck, he would manage to escape the security forces afterwards.

Probably.

The Pan slowed the SE2 still further. One of the pursuing security forces vehicles finally caught up and pulled alongside. The Grongle officer at the window sternly pointed down, indicating to the parking area behind the Botanical Gardens below them. Presumably, he wanted The Pan to land there.

'Arnold's Y-Fronts, I hope this works,' said The Pan, and did as the officer ordered.

As he came in to land, he was careful to select a place where there was just enough room to take off again. He slowed to a stop. Should he retract the wings? No, but they might not fall for it if he didn't. With a worried sigh he pressed the button. There was a quiet whine as the wings melded back into the side of the vehicle. He left the engine running and waited.

The security force's snurds pulled up behind him.

Wait for it.

The officers who'd seen The Pan and used the facial recognition software on him climbed out and walked towards him. One had a machine gun and the other two had laser pistols at the ready.

Still wait.

He checked the ordnance on the snurds behind him. They were the modern ones with lasers. The noses of a row of APTs—all purpose torpedoes—were clearly visible behind the grille at the front of the nearest one.

'Just my luck,' The Pan muttered.

The Grongles fanned out, two covering him, the one with the machine gun and one of the others with a laser pistol. The third strolled nonchalantly towards the snurd.

Wait for it.

The officer bent down then raised his hand to knock on the window.

Now!

In a plume of tyre smoke, The Pan sped away, pressing the button to activate aviator mode. As soon as he could, he took off. He hadn't left as much room as he'd thought and the back wheels of the SE2 squeaked as they bumped the roof of another snurd parked in its path. It wasn't enough to slow the SE2 down though, and it carried on climbing steeply into the sky.

The Pan checked his watch again. Seven minutes. Arnold's earwax! This was going to be tight. The officers on the ground were only just getting airborne, but unfortunately they hadn't been as greedy as The Pan hoped. Security forces and police vehicles rose up from the surrounding streets like angry insects, seven of them.

'Smeck,' he muttered.

Stuff smooth driving. He'd just have to protect the pastry as best he could.

Chapter 4
Delivery

Machine-gun fire peppered the side of a nearby building, along with laser fire from the more modern police snurds.

'Arnold's trousers!' The Pan shouted as he rolled the SE2 to avoid it. There were ten on his tail now. All the while he held the box containing the pastry with one hand, keeping it upright and trying to cushion it from the worst excesses of his evasive manoeuvres. He zig-zagged between two buildings and under a portico, throwing his pursuers for just long enough to cruise past the first-floor windows. If his calculations were correct, the window he wanted was the second one along. He wound down the windows, opened the roof, undid his seat belt and levelled the snurd out. Then, at what he hoped was the right moment, he pressed the self-park button so the SE2 wouldn't crash, leapt up, grabbing the pastry as he did so and dived through the window of the building. It was a great plan but it would have hurt less if the window had actually been open.

The Pan held out one arm to cushion his landing. He was going too fast to stop. Instinctively, he rolled to slow himself to a more controllable speed, lobbing the cake box into the air as he did so, because it was the only way to keep it even vaguely level. He managed to catch it by the ribbon as he stood up. Round a table, a group of assorted beings in business suits stared at him in silence. They were all elderly. Lawyers, The Pan suspected, or possibly accountants, maybe both; three males and one female. If they were surprised they hid it with consummate skill.

One of the males raised his eyebrows. He was a Galorsh,

one of K'Barth's mountain species. He had a dog like face with spaniel-like purple ears. He would have a long tail too, The Pan knew, but it was currently hidden from view. He was covered in a coat of thick, luxuriant purple fur. Unlike the smaller furry genera, Galorshes and their other mountain counterparts, Blaggysomps, usually wore clothes over the top of their fur. This Galorsh was wearing a dark suit, as were his male human comrades. But where the two other males wore straight ties, he sported an immaculate dark blue bow tie with white spots. A set of half-moon spectacles perched on the end of his long nose.

'Sorry to drop in like this. Rest assured, you're not in any danger,' said The Pan. He noticed the sound of approaching police sirens. 'Although I might be. Um, may I ask which of you is Arnhelm Gaspot?' The smartly attired Galorsh raised a purple furry hand. 'Great. This is from Mister Big Merv, with his very best wishes on the eve of Arnold's birth,' said The Pan. He bowed and deposited the box on the table in front of Mr Gaspot with a flourish.

'That was quite some entrance. You should get a job with the circus.'

'Thank you.'

'Would you mind opening the box, young man?'

Blimey! There wasn't time for this. 'Of course. My pleasure,' said The Pan politely. With half an ear listening for sounds of pursuit from outside, he undid the ribbon and lifted the lid.

As expected, 'the package' was a pastry effigy of Arnold, The Prophet, stuffed full of confectioner's custard, because that was the food K'Barthans traditionally exchanged with their friends and family on this particular day. But The Pan had never seen one so ornately decorated. Instead of hundreds and thousands to denote The Prophet's hair, this one was covered in squirls of dark chocolate. Around it were garlands of flowers and leaves all sculpted out of sugar icing. In the centre, underneath the face, was a decorated sugar icing plaque bearing one of the sayings of The Prophet, a popular one for his birth celebrations about how beings should all be decent to one another. It was a wonder to behold. But the most amazing thing about it, to The Pan, was that none of the bits had broken off. Mrs Dingleton had said it was some of her best work. She was correct on so many levels but The Pan also felt a tiny inkling of pride that he'd delivered it safely.

Arnhelm Gaspot was tearing up, which was touching, but only going to delay things at a point when the rising cacophony of sirens from the street confirmed that a sharp exit was essential. The sirens stopped abruptly just outside, with an accompaniment of screeching tyres. Yes. It was definitely time to go.

'I think I'd better be off,' said The Pan as the sounds of vehicle doors being slammed shut and Grongle police officers yelling the odds at one another rose up from the street below.

'Will you not have a slice of Big Merv's pastry with us?' asked Arnhelm Gaspot.

'Normally, I would be honoured. Today, I'm afraid I have an urgent appointment elsewhere,' gabbled The Pan, speaking as quickly as he could while still keeping his words intelligible.

'Ah of course, more pastries to deliver,' said one of the others, the lady.

'Exactly, ma'am,' lied The Pan.

Arnhelm nodded and The Pan caught a quick exchange of glances between him and the others. 'As you wish.'

'Thanks. I wonder if you could point the way to the roof?'

Wordlessly all four of them pointed to a door in the corner marked 'Fire exit'. Then Arnhelm said, 'I believe the stairs are through there.'

'Thanks.' The Pan ran half way across the room and turned back. 'I'd hide the pastry if I were you. There are some Grongles following me who might not like the sentiment.'

After all, celebrating The Prophet's Birthday *was* illegal, even if everyone was doing it.

****

As soon as the young man had disappeared though the door to the fire escape, Arnhelm Gaspot put the lid back on the cardboard box, hastily tied up the ribbons and passed it to his friend and associate of fifty years, Norton Creepal.

With an arthritic 'oof,' Norton passed it to his colleague Bunday, who bent down and pushed the box out of sight under the folds of the floor-length damask tablecloth with his foot. Then someone else burst in through the remains of the window; a Grongle security forces trooper, followed by two colleagues.

'You people seem to be going to an awful lot of trouble. There's a perfectly good door, you know,' said Norton.

'Shut up, non-being, we aren't "people"—we're Grongles. Where did he go?'

'The fellow with the box?'

'No. Arnold, The Prophet and fifteen acolytes.'

There was a short silence while Arnhelm thought about saying something withering, or worse, sarcastic. It was tempting but there'd be ramifications, and he really couldn't brook the prospect of waiting a moment longer than necessary to tuck into the pastry that was hidden under the table.

'That way,' he said, pointing, not to the fire exit, but to a set of double doors behind him which led onto a gallery around the hotel's central atrium.

'Come on boys,' shouted the Grongle and he and his three colleagues ran off.

Arnhelm, Norton and their two friends Bunday and Greenon sat in silence for a moment, listening to the sound of footsteps receding along the gallery and shouts in the hall below. Then all was quiet. They sat for a few more moments, waiting. Nothing else happened.

'Well, that seems to be about that,' said Arnhelm, rubbing his hands together.

'Mmm, cake time,' said Bunday with a wink. He leaned down and pulled the box out from under the table.

The hall outside rang with harsh shouts and the four colleagues could hear more security forces vehicles arriving, sirens blaring.

'I do wish they'd shut off that racket, I can't hear myself think,' sighed Arnhelm.

'Our delivery man has form presumably,' said Bunday.

'I suppose, or maybe they knew he was carrying a Prophet's Birthday pastry.'

'It seems like an awful lot of police for just that,' said Greenon thoughtfully.

'I expect he's just been unlucky,' said Bunday.

'Then the poor boy is uncannily unfortunate, I'd say,' sighed Greenon, smoothing her bouffant hair with one hand.

'Well not really, he was breaking the law.'

'She has a point though Bunday, old chap. There are millions of beings breaking the law all over the city at present. I mean, look at us,' said Arnhelm. Norton agreed.

'I did wonder if I should suggest he get under the table with the pastry,' said Arnhelm.

'Oh no, no, he's Big Merv's man. He'll be far too proud to involve us,' said Greenon.

'Agreed. He knows the correct etiquette,' said Bunday.

'They're probably after him for something else,' said Norton. 'hazard of the job in his line of work, I'd say.'

The yelling and shouting in the halls continued, along

with the sound of heavy boots clumping up and down the stairs and occasionally, across the floor of the room above.

'Crikey! I wish they'd pipe down or go search somewhere else!' grumbled Greenon.

'Quite! It sounds as if they are searching the whole bally hotel!' said Bunday.

'Much good may it do them! I'd bet our lad is long gone.'

'Still, we'd best get stuck in,' said Arnhelm. 'We don't want to be caught with contraband. We should eat the evidence as quickly as possible.' He rubbed his hands together.

'Excellent plan, Arnhelm,' said Greenon. 'I'll call for a knife.'

Arthritic knees cracking, she heaved herself slowly to her feet, but such was her anticipation at the thought of eating the delicious pastry that she was almost sprightly as she made her way over to the bell on the wall and pressed it.

'Don't forget the plates,' said Bunday.

Arnhelm had another look in the box. 'We'll need forks, Greenon. I bet my bottom there'll be more confectioner's custard than any of us can shake a stick at in the middle of that pastry!'

'Does Big Merv still use Mrs Dingleton's?' asked Norton.

'Oh yes, nothing but the best for him,' said Arnhelm with a chuckle.

'Marvellous! You can't get better cakes than Dingleton's!' said Bunday.

As Norton and Arnhelm set about opening the pastry box again the manager arrived. He was clearly flustered.

'So sorry gentlemen,' he nodded at Greenon, 'and madam, we've had a little bit of trouble. Nothing … to … worry … about …' His voice faded almost to a whisper as he saw the windows.

All four elderly beings turned and followed his gaze.

'Yes,' said Norton. 'We had a little of that ourselves. As a result, it's getting a bit nippy in here. Can you close the shutters for us? There's a good fellow.'

The manager rallied magnificently. 'Certainly sir, one moment.' He walked out and they heard him call from the gallery, 'Fenton, Smelchet, Abarth, come up here and close these shutters. Pronto ladies.' He reappeared. Three small red furry monopeds—Blurpons; Fenton, Smelchet and Abarth presumably—followed hotly on his heels.

'Is there anything else I can get you?' he asked.

'Just a knife, four plates and four cake forks,' said Arnhelm.

'And a bottle of bubbly would be nice!' Bunday chipped in.

'And some coffee to warm us up,' said Greenon.

'Certainly,' said the manager.

Chapter 5
Unexpected help

The Pan ran up the stairs, three at a time, eager to press his advantage. So far, no-one was following. Maybe the old gimmers had helped him out and sent the Grongles the wrong way. Possibly. He shouldn't bank on it though. Since he spent a lot of time running The Pan was fit, but by the time he reached the eighth floor, even he was beginning to flag. He slowed to take stock and looked up the hollow stairwell. Only another four to go he reckoned.

They'll go up in the lift. They're probably overtaking you right now, said a miserable little voice in his head. 'Piss off,' he gasped as he struggled on.

A door banged below.

'Check the roof!' shouted a voice.

'Why would he be up there?'

'The snurd, you moron! Did you see it crash after he jumped out of it?'

'No, but—'

'Exactly! It must have self park. He'll be calling it back.'

Hmm, that one sounded a little smarter than the usual; smart enough to guess The Pan's cunning escape plan, even if, as plans went, it wasn't all that cunning. He could hear the Grongles bickering with one another as they started clattering up the stairs towards him. With legs like lead from the running he'd already done and shaking with fear, The Pan skittered stealthily up one more floor and slipped through a half-open fire exit into the corridor beyond.

He walked purposefully along the hall, as if he was meant to be there, trying desperately not to sound as out of breath as he was—or actually wheeze. He had a back-up plan but it depended if anyone was in their room. At just after four pm they might not be. And even if they were, he had to persuade them to let him walk through their bedroom to the balcony and summon his snurd.

The hotel was built in a square round a central atrium and a corridor with rooms either side ran along each side of the square. As The Pan rounded a corner, he realised that the beds on this corridor were being made up. That was a worry. The staff might cause a problem, especially since these ones were Blurpons. Blurpons were similar to look at to Spiffles, but they were the polar opposite in character. They were red and furry, with cat-like features, hands rather than paws and one foot. Being unipedal didn't hinder them at all, especially in a fight. Blurpons were famous for two things; their unsurpassed skill at the laundering arts and a tendency to be utterly, psychotically violent. Oh yes, and there was a third thing for which they were famous; the ease with which they took offence. The Pan knew that the worst thing he could do to a Blurpon was mention size or tell it that it looked cute (even if it did). He'd wake up in hospital. In fact, any kind of communication with Blurpons was fraught with the kind of 'difficulties' that might result in a trip to hospital or, at the least, substantial injury. Yep. He'd have to play this carefully … or maybe pick another corridor. No, the pursuit would soon reach the roof, find it empty and come looking. If he wanted to escape he had to get in to a room, fast.

The two Blurpons with the trolley of clean sheets and towels gave him a bit of a look as he squeezed past. He was careful not to touch any of the laundry—it might make them cross and he really, really didn't want to do that.

'Ah, here we are,' he said cheerfully to the third Blurpon, who was blocking the doorway of an empty room. 'This is mine, ninety three b, yes?'

The Blurpon gave him a bit of a look and didn't move aside. 'No. This is room ninety three a.'

Arse.

A door slammed in the distance.

'We are conducting a search,' boomed a voice in the corridor from which The Pan had just come. It seemed the Grongles had brought their megaphone inside with them. 'There is a dangerous felon on the loose. Stay in your rooms and cooperate fully and you've nothing to fear.'

The Blurpon looked up at The Pan with an enquiring expression and groomed its whiskers casually. 'Dangerous?' it asked him.

'No. It's complicated. I was delivering pastries and—'

'Neldop! Waldron! Can you come here a minute?' the Blurpon spoke across him.

The other two came and stood behind The Pan blocking his escape. He was trapped. He wasn't a fighter. He knew he couldn't take on one Blurpon, let alone three. He looked into the room. He could see the window, beyond which lay the balcony and escape. His snurd was out there, waiting, if he could persuade the Blurpons to let him through.

'If you could turn a blind eye I'd be over that balcony and out of your life in a trice.'

'That will be difficult,' said the Blurpon. The Pan couldn't be absolutely sure—and it would be certain death to ask—but he suspected this one was a lady. Not that it made much difference. Both genders of Blurpon were as psychotic as each other. Although, this one didn't sound angry or even surprised to find a young man trying to escape through one of the hotel's rooms; she merely came over as firm.

The Pan wondered if he should try dropping to his knees and begging. No. The Blurpon might take it as an effort to get down to her level. Blurpons were notoriously chippy about their size and he wasn't going to test the theory.

'If you jump out of that window,' the Blurpon explained, 'they will question whether or not we saw you and,' she shrugged, 'turned a blind eye.'

'What if you say I overpowered you and got past?' asked The Pan hopefully.

The Blurpon looked him up and down. 'We have to tell them something vaguely believable.'

In his nervousness, The Pan almost laughed at that. Instead he smiled wanly at her. 'Fair point,' he said. Now what? They weren't going to dob him in, were they? He said nothing more. He felt instinctively that he should wait a second and see what the Blurpon did next. She seemed to be unusually laid back for her species, either that or she was messing with him. No, surely not. Maybe she just hated the Grongles that little bit more than she hated everyone else. With the security forces rapidly approaching, The Pan couldn't help fidgeting restlessly. After a short pause, which felt like an eternity, the Blurpon spoke up again.

'I think we can get you out of the hotel without compromising ourselves, and it'll be worth it just to annoy those clodhopping smeckers,' she waved an arm towards the end of the corridor, where the sounds of the Grongles approaching was getting louder. 'Neldop, get the trolley in here, can you?'

The sound of doors banging, boots clumping and orders being shouted in Grongolian came from along the hall.

'Quick, they're coming! They'll be on us any minute,' said one of the Blurpons, Waldron, The Pan thought it was, as, together with her colleague Neldop she dragged a large trolley into the room. At the front of the trolley, shelves towered to a height of about five feet with neatly folded clean laundry on them; bed linen, crisp white towels and bath mats with a pot of the free toiletries the hotel provided. Behind the shelves, to the front of the trolley, was a framework with a huge linen bag attached to it which was full of dirty sheets. Clearly, it was designed for bigger species but someone had attached a ladder up one side and there were grab handles fixed to the shelves in order to allow smaller beings to climb up and down them. Although the average Blurpon can jump at least twice their height so The Pan presumed they used them for hanging on, rather than actually climbing. As if to answer his thoughts the head Blurpon jumped easily into the trolley. She tossed a bunch of the used linen out onto the bed before bouncing out again.

Arnold's bottom! The Pan could hear the sound of Grongolian jackboots marching closer.

The Blurpon's dark eyes met his. 'In you get,' she said.

The Pan didn't hang around. Jumping into the sack he lay still in the bottom. He felt the weight of more sheets landing on top of him and then movement as the trolley was hauled back into the hall straight into the path of the approaching Grongles.

'You there, what are you doing?' demanded one of the Grongles. They were all speaking Grongolian, of course. None of them ever bothered to speak Tithian, the language of K'Barth.

'We're changing the sheets,' replied the Blurpon, also in Grongolian, with what sounded like purposefully bad pronunciation. 'Or at least we're attempting to. Some scrawny little git in a hat just ran past and nearly knocked the trolley over. It was only Waldron and Neldop's swift action that saved the clean laundry. Do you know how long it would take us to go and get more, load up the trolley again and—'

'Save it for someone who gives a toss, non-being,' growled the Grongle in charge.

'Yeh, we don't give a smeck about your sheets, vermin,' said one of the others. The Pan could almost feel the

Blurpon bristling with irritation from where he was hidden. Fair play though, because if the Blurpons were angry, none of them did anything. That, in itself, was amazing.

'Which way did he go?' demanded the Grongles.

There was a slight pause as if the Blurpons were pretending to wrestle with their consciences and then The Pan heard the leader of the three say, 'That way.'

'Stand aside!' shouted the Grongles and The Pan felt the trolley bump as the Grongle shoved it out of his path and barged past. Their progress along the corridor was marked by the sounds of shouts, the thumps and bangs of furniture being overturned, and smashing porcelain.

'Arnold's hair, I'm so tempted to thump those snot-coloured hooligans,' muttered the nameless Blurpon. 'There's a genuine Murdle Snork vase on the landing. So rare, and it's survived two hundred years in a hotel, for Arnold's sake. What's the betting those blundering idiots smash it? I wouldn't mind them systematically stripping this country of its artworks if they actually showed the smallest hint of appreciation for a single one of the items they're taking. But they don't! They're just a bunch of philistines collecting it all like marbles to annoy us.'

Clearly, in this case, it was working.

'I'm sure it'll survive,' said one of the others (it sounded like Waldron but The Pan couldn't be sure).

'It'd better.'

'You and your art stuff,' Neldop chided gently.

The Blurpon art lover huffed in annoyance as the trolley trundled along to the next room. 'Blame my predecessor. He's a real expert though. Before I was promoted, he kept pointing out all the artworks in this hotel as we passed them. I suppose it's rubbed off.'

'It still makes you unusual,' said Waldron.

'I know it's weird. But he was so enthusiastic, I feel I

have to look after them for him now,' said the leader.

'We didn't say it was a bad thing,' said the Waldron as the trolley stopped. The Pan felt it wobble while one of the Blurpons jumped on and off it, removing clean sheets and towels from the shelved part.

A few moments later he felt a set of sheets being added to the pile of dirty ones on top of him and then he heard a voice, closer to, as the un-named Blurpon leaned in towards him and whispered. 'Stay where you are. You're not going to get out of here without trouble unless we help you.' Then in a louder voice she said, 'Ladies, this bag's filling up a bit fast. The chute's only at the end of the corridor so I'd say it makes sense to do it now.'

'Yeh. Good plan. We don't have a spare though,' said Waldron. 'We'll have to empty this one out and put it back.'

'You happy doing that, girls?'

'Course we are,' said Neldop.

Once again, closer to The Pan, the Blurpon whispered, 'We'll put you down the chute with the laundry. Don't worry, I've been down that chute myself. We take it in turns—one poor blighter has to drag the trolley back to the hotel laundry at the end of service but the rest of us go down the chute! It's fun.'

'It is?' whispered The Pan.

'Oh yes, it's a blast! If we're halfway through we just empty the bag into the chute, but in this instance, I'll go first, just so my colleagues in the laundry aren't unduly surprised by you. You'll land in a bin of soft towels and I'll let you out the back when the coast's clear. You'll be on your way home in no time.'

The Blurpon was as good as her word.

The Pan felt the laundry being swiftly removed from on top of him. 'Ready?' said a voice—not Neldop or Waldron but the other one, the art lover who also appeared to be in charge.

'Yeh.'

'The coast's clear,' said one of the others.

'Right, let's go.'

The Pan climbed out of the trolley just in time to see the small red furry form of the first Blurpon disappearing through a small two-way door, like a cat flap, or the lid of a swing bin, which was mounted in the wall.

'Thanks ladies,' he whispered hurriedly to the other two, before diving down after their leader.

There followed about ten seconds of some of the rankest fear The Pan had ever felt. He heard the joyous whoops of the Blurpon ahead of him and the sound of somebody else screaming at the top of their lungs as the pair of them fell through the blackness. Luckily the terrified screaming didn't last long as The Pan realised where it was coming from and managed to shut himself up. The next moment he landed with a soft squish onto a pile of dirty laundry.

'Woah,' he said shakily as he looked up.

He was in a huge laundry bin. Above him, a line of three red furry Blurpon faces were ranged along the edge staring at him. The one who'd come down the chute with him held out a hand and helped him to his feet.

'Wasn't that wonderful?' she said.

'Yeh, it was certainly ... something,' said The Pan.

He followed his new friend over the side of the container and stood against a nearby wall for a moment while his beats per minute returned to more acceptable levels, his legs began to feel less wobbly and his hands stopped shaking.

'If you wait here with my esteemed colleagues for a moment,' said the Blurpon. She was definitely way more laid back than average for her species, although her 'esteemed colleagues' were totally in keeping with The Pan's preconceptions of Blurpon ferocity and scariness.

'Hi,' squeaked The Pan. They said nothing but continued to stare menacingly.

'Don't mind them,' said the other Blurpon, his saviour. The Pan watched her open the fire door and look out. She took her time checking. Something about the methodical approach with which she surveyed the scene outside made The Pan wondered if she'd rescued others.

'Jolly dee. It's all clear. On you go,' she said.

The Pan walked shakily over to join her.

'How can I ever thank you?' he said.

'Make the risk we just took worth it. Don't get caught.'

The Pan nodded. 'I'll try,' he said and stepped out into the winter dusk.

****

The Pan of Hamgee slipped quietly and anonymously out of the Garden View Hotel and made his way in the direction of the up-and-coming quayside area where Big Merv's night club, The Big Thing, was situated. Luckily Big Merv was elsewhere on 'important business' so The Pan managed to avoid another buttock-clenchingly scary debrief from Big Merv himself. Instead, he was able to report to Roberta, chauffeur and bar lady, also known as Bob. This made things a lot easier, not to mention faster. She handed The Pan a bundle of notes from the till, more than last time he noticed (or maybe that was just because Bob was the one paying him rather than her boss).

'I gather you had a bit of trouble,' she said conversationally as she handed over the cash.

'Nothing I couldn't handle,' lied The Pan.

'Yeh, right,' said Bob, with a wink. She clearly saw straight through The Pan's bravado. The Pan didn't care—it was all what Big Merv would have called, 'puff and wind,' anyway.

The Grongles would give up on him soon enough but for

now the search was still on. So he had to take a circuitous route to Mrs Dingleton's bakers to pick up the pastries. He only just made it by five, but to his delight the shop was still open.

'I'm so glad you came back,' Mrs Dingleton said when he walked through the door. 'These will be past their best by tomorrow so I'm loathe to waste them.'

'I'm sorry to add to your trouble but … would you be able to separate six from the rest? After this afternoon, I owe somebody a favour. I thought these would be a good way to thank them.'

Mrs Dingleton's beady black eyes met The Pan's. He had a feeling he was being read, and read well. Then again, she probably realised he was on the run. He'd benefited from her 'feeding the ducks' on the quay before now. She'd know he was pond slime, at best, on Ning Dang Po's complicated scale of social importance.

'Of course, wait here.' She bustled off into the back of the shop and a few minutes later, returned with four boxes. 'Now then, I had a few other leftovers today, just a handful, so I've put a riser in the boxes and a couple of those on top. For appearance's sake, you understand.' She lined up the three original boxes along the top of the counter. 'This one,' she said, adding another slightly smaller box to the pile, 'contains the ones you asked me to separate out.'

'Do you have a pen?' he asked her.

She handed one over and he scrawled a message across the cardboard lid of the last, smaller box. Five Zloty note at the ready, he double checked with Mrs Dingleton how much he owed her but she just waved him away. After a moment of wrestling with his conscience, which put up only token resistance and was quickly overcome, he thanked her and left the shop, with his boxes.

You don't have to do this, he thought.

'No, I do,' he answered aloud. The Pan hated putting himself in harm's way but at the same time, when he turned towards the Parrot and Screwdriver he felt that sinking feeling that told him he couldn't head there quite yet. It was only just after five pm but, it being midwinter, it was already dark and cold outside. He heartily wished he could just head to the pub but it was no good, first, he was going to have to Do The Right Thing.

Arnold's nostril hair.

He'd be late, and although they would understand, Gladys and Ada would probably give him a right ear bashing.

Never mind. Needs must.

Chapter 6
Doing the Right Thing

With a sigh, The Pan summoned his wheels and put the three larger pastry boxes in the boot. He removed his cloak and hat and used them to wedge the boxes firmly in position. Then he put the smaller one in the front seat, drove round the corner and parked in an alley.

Some days earlier, The Pan had bought a disguise of sorts. Now seemed as good a time as any to try it out. He took a spray-can of grey hair dye from where he'd stored it under the front seat, and removed some aviator shades from the glove compartment. Only a numpty would wear sunglasses after dark, but The Pan didn't have much choice—it was definitely best he looked a little different. He removed his warm velvet jacket and took off his virulently patterned paisley shirt, leaving just the white t-shirt he was wearing as a vest underneath. After a quick glance at the freezing streets outside, he put the jacket on again.

Next, he sprayed liberal amounts of the hair dye into his hair and combed it through. Finally, he took out a pot of foundation and rubbed it over his face. He checked his reflection in the side mirror of the snurd. Yeh, that definitely looked … different. It wasn't a very credible mix of styles, the shirt and jacket were too young for the shades and hair, he looked like an ageing rock star with issues about his lost youth. On the other hand he was amazed and pleased to see that he didn't look like The Pan of Hamgee anymore.

'Mmm, this might work,' he muttered as he slipped back into the driving seat of the snurd and swiped his thumb over the fingerprint reader on the dash.

'Fingerprint ident accepted,' it said, in its sultry electronic voice and the engine started.

He drove down the back alleys and residential streets to the bottom of Waterfront Road, successfully avoiding any trouble. Then, regretfully, he got out of the snurd with the smaller cake box in hand. He pressed the self-park button and watched as the SE2 drove swiftly away into the night before starting to walk towards the Garden View Hotel.

The hotel seemed quiet and things there back to normal. Maybe the Grongles had given up on him. Hopefully. Despite the fact he was quaking with fear, he decided to be brazen, marching up the steps and into the lobby as if he was a perfectly normal law-abiding citizen, and owned the place.

'Can I help you sir?' asked the receptionist.

'You had a team of Blurpons changing the beds on the ninth floor this afternoon. I'm not sure what they were *all* called but I can name two: Neldop and Waldron. I was wondering if you could give them these.' He held out the box. 'They and their three friends downstairs provided me with such excellent service during my stay that I wish to thank them.'

'Which room were you in?'

'Ninety three b.'

'Do you not mean ninety three a?'

Aaaargh!

'Well, yes and no,' The Pan rapidly backtracked. 'We had this running joke. Please tell them these are from the gentleman in ninety three b because then they'll understand exactly which guest it is.'

'Any other message? Apart from thank you?'

Smecking Arnold! She'd probably pressed a panic button and was keeping him talking until— no, no, calm, breathe, she wasn't, he told himself. He gave her what he hoped was a confident smile.

'No, no message. They'll know who I am,' he said.

She took the box with no further questions and The Pan turned tail and walked out as quickly as he could without appearing to move suspiciously fast or actually run. Potentially, he was courting disaster. His earlier antics had caused a security alert, after all. Sometimes it didn't matter, The Pan suspected the strength of the Grongles' reaction to any 'outrage', as they called it, depended as much on the identity of the officer in charge as the severity of the incident.

Sometimes, they acted as if they really couldn't be bothered. There would be a lot of officious posturing and 'measures'—a curfew, roadblocks or a couple of officers conducting desultory searches—but nothing much would *happen* and everything would return to normal very quickly. Other times, the security forces and police would get jumpy. Then they'd drag off pretty much any K'Barthan they happened across to 'help' with their enquiries, a process that involved, among other things, presenting a valid ID (which The Pan didn't have). His disguise would probably work but if he was asked to 'help' the punishment for lacking ID was being blacklisted.

'Mmm, double jeopardy,' he said.

Perhaps his line of thought was unconsciously making him act shiftily, or perhaps he was just unlucky. Whatever it was, as The Pan turned down a nearby street, he realised he was being shadowed by three members of the Grongolian security forces.

Arnold's eyebrows, not now! Hadn't they better things to do with their time? Never mind, he'd throw them off soon enough. But for the moment he had to pretend he was totally legitimate and normal. Only a criminal would notice he was being followed. The Pan must pretend he hadn't realised. He headed for Fuller's Row, a long street of once grand properties which were mostly derelict these days. Some were awaiting demolition, while others still housed the last few sitting tenants who had yet to be persuaded to leave. Doubtless some Grongolian consortium would bulldoze them soon enough and replace them with a ritzy, modern glass and steel skyscraper full of the kind of luxury apartments that only other Grongles could afford. The K'Barthans who'd lived there would have to move to another neighbourhood. For the moment, Fuller's Row presented The Pan with the only viable means of escape.

He would have to avoid the few houses that were still occupied. If he strolled into one of the derelicts as if it were his own, perhaps the Grongles following him would be persuaded he lived there—at least long enough for him to walk to the back door, out into the garden, nip over the back wall and get a decent start on them. It depended what kind of lock the door had. Picking pockets was one thing, but picking locks was much more difficult and not The Pan's forte. There was a certain kind of lock which could be unlatched by slipping a blade down the side of the door. Hopefully these houses were old enough to have one of those. The Pan didn't have a blade, of course, but he had a plastic pass to the lido in Hamgee which may have been five years out of date but was still very useful in these sorts of situations.

He picked a house. Not too obviously lived in but not too rundown either. Derelict was one thing but if he was really going to carry this off it did, at least, have to have a roof. The cast-iron gate was stiff and closed behind him with a clang as he marched up the path to the door, as if, well yes, as if he owned it. It was only as he tried the door handle that he realised he'd made an error.

Arnold's pants, someone lives here! he thought as he realised there was a dim light shining through the grimy stained glass panes in front of him. How could he have managed to pick one of the only ones with a smecking inhabitant? The sunglasses. That's how.

Idiot.

He made a mental note not to wear them after dark in future. Fleetingly, he wondered if he had time to vault over the railings and pretend to 'live' in the house next door but a quick check behind him up the street, using the useful eyes in the back of his head, revealed the dark shapes of three Grongles turning the corner. He could try and see if he could get in, but if anything went wrong, he would just be handing them an excuse to arrest him.

Arse. Now what?

Maybe the person actually living in the house would take pity on him. The Pan knocked on the door, hoping against hope that whoever inhabited these dingy premises would open it after dark. Fat chance! Especially on the eve of The Prophet's Birthday. They were probably having a similar clandestine celebration to Gladys and Ada at the Parrot and Screwdriver. For a moment, The Pan thought longingly of his friends. He had to get back there. Why in the name of The Prophet hadn't he quit while he was ahead? The only sensible course of action after the afternoon's chase was to avoid Waterfront Road for several days. What had possessed him to traipse all the way back to the hotel with those pastries? Why had he tried to do The Right Thing? He was stupid, that's why.

He bent down and peeped through the letterbox. It was an ordinary hall with a chequerboard floor in red and blue tiles, clean and swept. The scene was dimly illuminated by a crack of light coming from a slightly open door to the reception room at the front of the house, on The Pan's right.

There was a table, upon which sat a wallet and a bunch of keys. In the gloom, The Pan could make out a set of stairs straight ahead of him. There was a passage leading past them to a back wall with a door. Through this, The Pan knew, there would be a long thin kitchen with a scullery on the end, a small backyard and beyond that, the back gate and freedom. The Grongles were getting closer. Should he tap on the window, The Pan wondered. No.

The Pan pretended to suffer a fit of coughing and as he did so, risked knocking on the door one more time, louder.

Come on, please, please answer.

'You there,' snapped a voice. Oh no. The Grongles had reached the gate.

With a sinking heart The Pan turned round, one hand pressed to his chest and said,

'Who? Me?'

'Yes. Is this your house?'

'Um ...' Arnold's sweaty sandals, now what? Lie, obviously. 'Yes.'

'Is it really?' said one of the Grongles, his voice loaded with the kind of sarcasm levels of which, usually, only a K'Barthan would be capable.

'Yes, I forgot my wallet, left it on the hall table, my keys too.'

The sarcastic Grongle opened the gate walked up the short path and joined The Pan on the doorstep. 'Show me.'

The Pan stepped to the side, opened the letterbox one handed and gestured to the gap it revealed.

The Grongle leaned down and looked in. 'It seems you're telling the truth.'

'Yes sir,' said The Pan in his best Grongolian. 'I wouldn't knowingly leave the house without my ID.'

'Then how come you're outside and you know it's in there?'

'Because I forgot to check my pockets and pulled the door to. You know how it is, I left my wallet and keys on the table. I only nipped out for a pint of milk, you see, but I didn't realise until I'd got to the paper shop and when I tried to pay I found that I—'

The Grongle, apparently unimpressed by The Pan's tissue of lies, took a static-powered, hand-held personal computer from his belt—standard army issue—and The Pan tried to keep a lid on his fear. Looking scared wouldn't help. There was no room to run here, but he might be able to later, possibly, if he lulled them into a false sense of security; kept calm and cooperated. Then, he could scarper when they least expected it. There was a long silence while the Grongle looked from the screen to The Pan and back again, first with a perplexed expression, and then with a look that suggested he thought all his birthdays had come at once.

'You're coming with me,' he said as he closed the case with a snap and put it back in a pouch on his belt.

'Are you sure? Only my ID is in there, with my keys and I—'

The Grongle unholstered his laser pistol, pointed it at The Pan and said, 'You're coming with me,' one more time.

The Pan cleared his throat and tried hide his fear.

'Right,' he said squeakily.

****

Not far away, in the Parrot and Screwdriver pub, Gladys, Ada and Their Trev definitely weren't celebrating The Prophet's Birthday, no, not at all. Gladys peered out from the doorway of the room behind the bar, the Holy of Holies as they called it, where they prepared the food and did the washing up. Ada was in there with her, helping prepare the meal, meanwhile Trev was manning the bar. The oven was rammed to the gunwales with assorted meat and fish dishes, the vegetables were roasting, the special soup was warming on the stove and the puddings of enchantment were floating, ready, in their bath of chocolate sauce—made with genuine Nectar of The Prophet chocolate procured on the black market, obviously, via one of the punters. None of that rubbishy fake Grongolian stuff in the shops.

'The Pan of Hamgee isn't here,' Gladys snorted. 'He'd be late for his own funeral, that one.'

'He did promise, Gladys dear, and he doesn't give his word lightly.'

'I dunno. I reckon he'll swear anything blind as gets him out of trouble.'

'Not to us.'

'I still reckons we has ter get on. 'S his fault if he misses a course or two cause he is late, the thoughtless little so and so! We has to get started, or we isn't going ter get it all in.'

'He'll miss the curried squid. Such a pity.'

'Ner, no-one else'll touch that an' I isn't wasting it. I reckons I'll serve it between the quail an' the pie and chips when we does the crackers. That gives him til eight.'

Ada smiled to herself. Gladys was only annoyed with The Pan because she was worried about him. The repositioned squid course was proof. He'd be forgiven at once when he arrived.

'I hears there's been a big bust-up in town.'

'Yes, Pub Quiz Alan and Psycho Dave have only just arrived and said there was trouble at the Garden View Hotel. Waterfront Road was cordoned off for an hour this afternoon apparently.'

'Yer. Trev mentioned that. He reckons we has some more "beer" coming in to deliver and all.' As Gladys said the word 'beer' she put one finger on the side of her nose. For all their apparent innocence, neither the two old ladies, nor Their Trev, were above a little clandestine activity, in this case smuggling. No-one suspected, of course, which made it a lot more straightforward than it might have been.

'That's the third lot this week!'

'Yer.'

'When.'

'Tomorrow.'

'D'you want this stirred, dear?'

'What?'

'The soup.'

Gladys gasped. 'What is I coming to? I forgot.'

'It doesn't matter. I remembered, and if I hadn't Trev would've done.'

'You isn't wrong there, he loves that soup does Trev. 'S his favourite course. Now, careful how you goes, with that, it doesn't want stirring too brisk. We doesn't want it going funny.'

'Quite, dear.'

'Humph! Remind me so I gets a fresh loaf out of the freezer. Those gannets out there is goin' ter eat everything that we has got,' said Gladys. But it was a satisfied 'Humph' Ada noticed, rather than an annoyed one. 'I dunno how our pre— pre— them lot who was doing this before us kept up with all the "beer".'

'Well they didn't, did they dear? They were arrested,' said Ada.

'Yer.'

'You don't think something has happened to him, do you?'

'The lad?' asked Gladys, meaning The Pan of Hamgee. She sucked the air through her teeth. Neither of them would ever admit it publicly, but the old ladies felt a keen sense of responsibility for The Pan.

'I was just thinking,' said Ada as she carried on stirring the soup. 'I suppose we shouldn't really be doing this with another delivery coming in. Not if we were sensible.'

'When was we ever sensible, Ada Maddox? 'S a bit late now.' Gladys chuckled. 'I doubts as anyone'll catch us.'

'Sometimes, I feel I ought to worry more. I wonder if we're being reckless.'

'Ner, 's more likely that we has got used to it.'

Gladys went to the window and looked out.

'Where is he?' said Ada.

'I dunno, but I is goin' ter give him a piece of my mind when he arrives. I reckons you can turn that off now.'

Ada switched off the gas and put the lid on the saucepan. There was a long silence. Gladys, still at the window, heaved a sigh.

'He'd be here, I know it. Something's happened to him,' said Ada.

'Yer.' Gladys heaved another sigh.

Ada and Gladys stood for a moment, in silence. Trev's deliveries, both legitimate and less so, took him all over the city, and that meant he was well connected. If there was anyone who could find out what had happened to The Pan of Hamgee, it would be Trev.

With a nod, Gladys went to the door of the Holy of Holies, 'Trev,' she called, 'is you able to pop in here for a minute?'

Chapter 7
Grim prospects

Arnold, The Prophet knew what the Grongle's personal computer had said about The Pan of Hamgee, but whatever it was, it wasn't good. One of the other two also drew his laser pistol and kept it trained on their prisoner while they escorted him back up the short path, out through the iron gate and into the street again. As the gate clanged shut, the third Grongle took a pair of handcuffs, putting one round The Pan's wrist and the other round his own.

'Are you sure this is strictly necessary?' asked The Pan as the Grongle grimly pulled him forward. 'Seriously, you don't need to be this thorough.'

'Yes, we do,' snarled the one handcuffed to him.

'No, really, I think there's been a mistake,' The Pan said, 'if you just leave me here I'll find a locksmith and be indoors in a jiffy.'

The one handcuffed to him stopped and one of the others stepped swiftly up, brandishing his laser pistol. The Pan cowered lower and further away from it as the Grongle wielding it approached. Finally he was brought up short by his handcuffed arm. The Grongle with the pistol slowly, purposefully, put the muzzle against The Pan's temple. He shuddered as he felt the cold metal touch his skin and screwed his eyes tight shut. Cold sweat began to seep out of his hairline. Arnold's bogies, there went any attempts to look calm and manly, worse, the dye in his hair would run. Please, please no.

'I'd think about it before you give us any more lip,' sneered the Grongle.

The Pan waited, crouched and trembling, until the Grongle took the gun away and then slowly, cautiously, he straightened up.

They didn't deign to acknowledge him after that. Instead, they spoke quickly and quietly among themselves. The Pan's Grongolian was a decent standard but it was hard to catch what was being said when they spoke in such fast low voices. Presumably they didn't wish him to eavesdrop. He could pick up a little though. It seemed they were going to walk him to the nearest police station on foot and they were arguing as to which one was closest. Arnold's conkers, if only he could pick the lock on the handcuff and make a run for it. However, while there was an outside chance of him opening a certain kind of locked door, handcuffs were well beyond him.

Eventually, they started to walk. The Pan didn't know where he was being taken—obviously, into police custody, but which police station? Where prisoners went made a difference. He followed his captors through the night and the few beings they encountered passed quickly by, heads down, not looking, not wanting to get involved. It was all The Pan could do not to beg for help, beg for mercy or just beg for his life but he suspected it wouldn't further his cause. He had to be sensible about this; he was still disguised, still wearing the stupid sunglasses, there might be hope.

The Grongles walked, in silence, for about ten minutes. Then, as they came out into a large open square, The Pan realised their destination. Across the wide expanse of cobbles, away on the other side, stood the Grongles' Security HQ; a building which had once been the Architrave's Palace, but which now served a far more sinister purpose. As the three Grongles dragged him onwards, towards it, The Pan slowed up, pulling on the handcuff, trying to make them stop.

'No,' he said.

The one handcuffed to him pulled him forward.

'No, no, no,' said The Pan, digging his heels into the cobbles, trying to get a purchase, tying to slow them down. 'Not in there, please.'

No-one ever escaped from the Security HQ. Any prisoners who went in there, literally, disappeared.

'Please, wait, can't we discuss this?' The Pan yanked at the handcuffs making absolutely zero impression on the Grongle attached to the end of his arm. 'For Arnold's sake! Please don't mislay me! You've got the wrong man. Please listen to me!'

Nothing. The three Grongles kept walking and The Pan, pulling and complaining on the handcuffs with increasing urgency skated and slithered over the cobbles as he tried to stay upright and, at the same time, stop them from moving.

'Please don't take me in there,' he whimpered.

Still they didn't dignify him with a reply but merely dragged him forward.

'I haven't done anything!' he cried, ignoring the existence of his extensive criminal record.

I don't want to die! thought The Pan. Arnold's socks, this was it, he was finally going to be mislaid, disappeared forever. He thought of Gladys and Ada, Their Trev and the punters at the Parrot and Screwdriver, waiting for him, wondering where he was. Arnold, he'd never see them again. And all those pastries in his snurd. Would it know where to take them? What was he thinking? The snurd would be fine and what did he care for the cakes? He'd be dead.

The only hope was his disguise. He wasn't dressed as The Pan of Hamgee. The Prophet knew it wasn't much but he clung to that hope because it was all he had.

'Please, please listen to me,' he begged, as the three

Grongles dragged him, inexorably, towards his doom. 'I mean no disrespect in talking to you,' he pleaded, 'but I—' And that's when the one who'd threatened him with a laser pistol, initially, ran out of patience and rounded on him.

'Shut up, vermin!' he snarled, drawing his weapon. He aimed and squeezed the trigger.

****

The Pan of Hamgee regained consciousness slowly. His fingertips and toes tingled muzzily and his head ached. He wasn't lying on the cobbled square. Oh no. Did that mean? Yes. They'd brought him inside while he was unconscious. He became aware of voices, Grongolian voices. It sounded as if they were arguing or at least debating something. Whatever it was they were doing, they didn't seem to be taking any notice of him for the moment, which he could only count as a relief.

He lay on the ground gathering his scattered wits. It seemed to be taking a long time. Then he felt someone put their arms under his, hauling him to his feet. Another one slapped his face, but not that hard. 'Ouch!'

'Good, you're awake.'

The Pan managed to persuade his legs to take his weight. He was still shaking, mostly from fear but being stunned with a laser pistol hadn't helped. Never mind, at least it was wearing off. He was indoors, in what appeared to be part of gothic undercroft converted into interrogation rooms. A quarter of a sturdy sandstone column made up one corner of the room, supporting a vaulted ceiling. The door was wooden and studded with nails, with a tiny barred window in it, traditional prison door style. The walls were whitewashed with sandstone brickwork cornices and corners left unpainted. At the back of the room was a window, set high up, with bars and sandstone mullions.

However, the thing that concerned him far more than his

surroundings was a Grongle looking into his face from a rather closer distance than he appreciated. Was this the one who'd slapped him? Probably.

The Pan concentrated, and finally his assailant's features swam into focus. He was clean shaven, youngish, with the dark black and red uniform of the security forces, with its occasional flash of white on the epaulettes, collar and cuffs. The Pan thought he was an officer—he wasn't brilliant at identifying rank though. After all, it didn't really make much difference if he was talking to a grunt or an officer in the grand scheme of things since they were all 'sir'. But he reckoned this one was a lieutenant, or possibly a captain. He was too young to have risen any higher than that, surely? As The Pan was mentally debating this he realised, to his dismay, that there was another one standing behind the Lieutenant, leaning against the wall by the door silently observing. That one had intelligence pips on his collar. Uh-oh. This was bad news.

'What's your name?' demanded the Lieutenant.

'The—' no wait a minute. *Don't tell him your real name you idiot!* 'Fred ...' The Pan cast about him for inspiration and latched onto the first thing he saw, the segment of sandstone pillar in the corner, 'Column, Frederick Column.' Arnold's armpits! Frederick Column? What kind of total moron was he? Still as The Pan took in his surroundings he realised it could have been worse. At least he hadn't called himself something really lame like Maurice Door, Gerald Table, Norbert Floor or, heaven forfend, Dennis Grongle.

'Permission to speak, Lieutenant, sir,' said one of the Grongles who'd brought The Pan in.

'Granted,' said the one who'd slapped him in the face to wake him up. The Pan looked past him, concentrating on the one behind, the one observing. He was tall, really tall, even for a Grongle; about six feet five. Nobody was taking any notice of him but it seemed to be a case of elephant-in-the-room style taking no notice. For all his apparent detachment from the scene being played out, the silent onlooker was clearly the one calling the shots. The Pan hadn't met an intelligence officer close up since his initial blacklisting—such was the reputation of the intelligence services that he'd made a concerted effort not to. Pity he had to meet one now.

'He has a criminal record, sir.'

'Yeh. He's a one-man crime wave, sir,' said one of the others.

The Pan looked down because he didn't want them to see his face, see that it was true. When he looked up again, the elephant-in-the-room one was staring straight at him.

'He's also blacklisted, as of three years ago in Hamgee.'

Smeck. They knew everything.

The Lieutenant turned to the Grongle standing behind him, who made no reply, but clearly communicated his wishes somehow.

'Shall we check?' he said.

What did it matter? The Pan thought morosely. This was the end of the road. Curtains. And yet ... they were arguing. And while they were arguing, surely there was still the tiniest, faintest sliver of hope.

The Lieutenant turned back to The Pan. As an officer, he had a smartphone rather than a personal computer. He held it up, pointing at The Pan. It made a fake electronic shutter-clicking noise as he took a photo.

There was a pause. It was probably not more than ten or fifteen seconds, but for The Pan it seemed like an eternity, as he bit down on his fear and panic and tried to remain calm. Eventually the Lieutenant turned to his silent escort with a perplexed expression.

'Sir, the whole system is down.'

'He's right, sir,' one of the three who'd arrested The Pan volunteered.

The silent observer finally spoke.

'Why?'

'It says power failure to the server, sir. It's booting up, so I'll wager it's fixed but it'll take a minute or two,' said the Lieutenant.

'Permission to speak, sir?' said one of the three who'd arrested The Pan.

'Go on,' said the Lieutenant.

'Sargent Benton, in reception, mentioned this. He said it was Captain Schprinkles who caused it. The power went out in the officer's mess and word is he tried to fix it himself and pulled out the wrong fuse.'

The Grongle standing by the doorway rolled his eyes and shook his head with a wry smile. It was an unnervingly normal gesture coming on the back of his previous impassivity.

'What did you say this felon's name was?' The Lieutenant asked one of the three who'd arrested The Pan.

'The Pan of Hamgee, sir.'

'Not ... Frederick Column?' asked the observing Grongle. His eyes met The Pan's, with an unfathomable expression, as one of the others answered,

'No, sir.'

The Lieutenant turned to The Pan. 'Where do you live, Mr Column?'

Mr Column? Did the fellow believe him? Surely not?

'Number twenty three, Fuller's Row,' said The Pan promptly, giving the address of the house he'd been 'pretending' to own when he'd been taken into custody.

'Postcode?'

'I'm terribly sorry, I don't know it, sir.'

'Never mind it'll be on your ID. Show me.'

'I can't, sir,' said The Pan, continuing hurriedly. 'I left my wallet and keys on the hall table. Stupid I know. I went back for them and that's when these fine soldiers of yours apprehended me.'

The Lieutenant was alert at once, as were the three grunts who'd arrested The Pan.

'Don't overdo it,' said the observing intelligence officer drily, completely unmanning The Pan by speaking in Tithian, the language of K'Barth. 'I know exactly what you K'Barthans think of my colleagues,' he added.

Arnold's smecking socks! What was going on?

'I—' began The Pan and stopped. There was an uncomfortable pause, since he could hardly argue with the truth. He took a deep breath, and despite being addressed in Tithian, he replied in Grongolian. 'I'm sorry, sir. Don't mind me, it's my nerves talking,' he said.

'Why would you be nervous, Mr Column?' asked the Lieutenant, jumping on the statement immediately.

'Unless you've something to hide,' sneered the one who'd originally handcuffed himself to The Pan.

The Pan shrugged. It was difficult to play it cool when he was shaking so much. Worse, he feared the cold sweat pouring from his temples really would be washing the grey dye out of his hair by now, or certainly any minute. Not that it mattered. Not that anything mattered, for this was surely the end of the road wasn't it? Yes, it had to be, except that something was off. The Pan didn't know what was going on but this was clearly not standard procedure. For all his pessimism and uncertainty the tiny spark of hope glowed feebly within him. He gathered up all his courage, took a deep breath and as politely and firmly, as he could, he said,

'Begging your pardon, sir, but you shot me,' to the Grongle who had done so, 'and while I concede it was only a stun shot and done with the best of intentions I'm sure, I confess it has made me a little nervous.'

Was that too ingratiating? The observing intelligence officer gave him a bit of an I've-already-warned-you-about-this look. Yes. Almost certainly. The Pan's voice trembled with fear as he spoke. He sounded like the biggest coward imaginable, but then again he was, so there was little point in trying to hide it. He was jittery and twitchy and it was all he could do to keep still. If only he could rake his hands through his hair but he dared not, because of the wretched dye. If the Grongles noticed he was wearing a disguise, however poor, they'd know for sure that he was up to no good, and he'd be really sunk.

'He does have a point, Corporal Plympton,' drawled the officer.

'Sir, Major, sir,' said the trigger happy get, or Plympton, as The Pan now knew he was called.

And then the Lieutenant's phone beeped.

'Tennant?' the intelligence officer, who The Pan had now learned was a major, addressed his colleague.

Lieutenant Tennant raised his eyebrows. 'This is strange, sir. There are two records, one that corresponds with what Corporal Plympton has said, and another that's incomplete ... How can that be?'

He passed the phone to his superior. There was silence as the Major consulted the screen, swiping from one record to the next.

'What do we do now, sir?'

'I'm not a being to go on appearances, but does he look dangerous to you?' asked the Major.

'I confess, no, sir,' said Plympton. 'But according to his record, he's a felon and no mistake.'

'If that *is* his record.' The Major frowned and consulted the smartphone in his hand a second time.

'He looks dodgy to me, sir.'

'Really?' The Major asked Plympton.

'Yessir. He also has three hundred and fifty counts of failing to stop for a police vehicle.'

Yeh well, that was probably about right, The Pan reflected. In fact, it might have been a bit on the low side.

'Yeeees,' said the Major absently as he consulted the screen. 'It says here, three hundred and fifty *three* counts of refusing to stop. You missed a few. Boys, that's a fair number. Who was that fellow last year? Running Sam they called him, didn't they? He held the record at twenty three. And look at all these annotations here.' The Major turned the screen towards them and waved a hand at it.

'He's also supposed to be helping us with our enquiries into seventy three counts of petty theft and one suspected count of breaking and entering, sir.'

That was definitely a low estimate. The Pan was surprised at how much of his thieving activity the Grongles appeared to have missed. The Major narrowed his eyes and gave The Pan a disbelieving look. 'How old are you?'

'I couldn't say sir, I'm an orphan,' replied The Pan—well, that much was true—'and I don't know, precisely, when I was born,' even if that wasn't.

Arnold in the skies! Not too many lies though or all this stuff would get too complicated to remember.

'I'll wager you have a rough idea?'

'What? When I was born?' The Pan asked, before he could stop himself.

'Yes, Mr Column,' said the Major heavily.

The Pan cleared his throat. 'Well, not exactly, but I think I'm about thirty seven.'

Was that old enough to have greying hair? He didn't dare make himself out as any older. Close up, like this, his youthful looks would betray the lie. After all, he was only young and he knew exactly when he was born, having been orphaned when he was sixteen rather than at birth the way he was asserting.

'And you say you left your ID in the house.'

'Yes sir, I was just returning to get it when your colleagues, here, arrested me.'

'Hmm.' There was silence as the Grongle looked at The Pan's record. 'Lads, that was good and diligent police work, but I'm afraid that what we have here is a computer malfunction.'

The one to whom The Pan had originally been handcuffed raised a tentative hand, but it was Corporal Plympton who answered.

'Sir, permission to speak, sir,' he said.

The Major waved a go-ahead hand.

'Are you sure, sir?'

'I'm afraid so lads. According to our Mr Column's interesting record, he is nineteen years old and was, apparently, blacklisted when he was sixteen.'

'Exactly, sir,' said Plympton.

'I don't think so.' The Major gave The Pan another look. Plympton and his friends were downcast and the Major continued, 'I ask you, in all fairness, do you think the pathetic creature in front of you could have survived three years?'

'It would account for the number of felonies, sir.'

'Very true, but it doesn't account for us. Can you see even the slipperiest, most inspired being keeping ahead of the power of the Grongolian security forces for that long?'

'Well ... when you put it like that, sir ...'

'I believe this fellow is telling the truth. I believe he *is* who he says he is but his record has somehow become corrupted or conflated with this Pan of Hamgee person's. Lindburg, Plympton, Handberg, you've all been highly methodical, exemplary even, and I can only sympathise. The reward on that other fellow, if he exists, would have been substantial.'

'Sir,' said Plympton miserably.

'Although since the record you cited listed him as blacklisted three years ago, I think we can safely assume it is rogue, an entry which wasn't closed correctly when the being in question was processed, perhaps.'

The Pan noted the word 'processed'—is that what they called disappearing people?

'Rogue, sir?' asked one of the others.

'Rogue.'

How did that happen? Not one of the Grongles had ever questioned The Pan's record in three years. Why was this one doing so now? It didn't make sense.

'But sir—'

Plympton was clearly thinking the same thing. He looked from the Major to The Pan and back, then shot a helpless appeal at the Lieutenant as the Major smoothly cut across him.

'I'm sorry to disappoint you. We've clearly all been the victims of a clerical error. Dodgy paperwork, if you will. I shall see that each of you receives a commendation and that the fool whose negligence has caused us so much trouble is identified, and pays for wasting our valuable energy and time.'

Was he bribing them with a commendation? It looked very much as if he was. No, surely not. Or at least, not knowingly, was he? This was weird.

'Yessir,' said Plympton and his mates. They sounded deflated, but not quite as badly as before.

'I'll take care of this being,' the Major said, gesturing dismissively to The Pan of Hamgee. 'You may go.'

With an air of defeated resignation, Corporal Plympton and his friends stood up and left the room.

Chapter 8
Deliverance

The Pan waited, trying to hide his blank incomprehension, not to mention his relief, in case the two remaining Grongles took it as a sign of guilt and changed their minds.

'Come with me,' the Grongle Major said.

The Pan looked up at the being towering above him. 'What? Now?'

'When else?' He nodded at the Lieutenant. 'Dismissed, Tennant,' he said.

Lieutenant Tennant saluted and stood aside as The Pan rose uncertainly to his feet and followed the Grongle Major into the corridor.

'Where are you taking me?' asked The Pan.

'You'll see soon enough,' he replied, in Tithian again.

No reassurance there, then. The Pan thought of making a run for it, but he realised that he couldn't escape in the Security HQ. Even if he managed to throw off his pursuit, he could never get out undetected. No, there was no escape right now, so he followed the Grongle along several corridors, down some stairs and ... hang on ... out into the entrance way.

'This is— are we—' he began but the Major silenced him with a look. 'Right,' he squeaked, following on in mute obedience. They went through the first of several security gates, came to a checkpoint and stopped.

'Hold out your right hand,' said the Major.

The Pan did as he was told. The Grongle clapped a handcuff round his wrist and fastened the other end to his own arm the exact same way his colleague had done earlier.

As he did so, he smiled reassuringly at The Pan, which merely served to unnerve him even more.

'Relax, Mr Column, this is just a formality,' he said as he checked it was fastened correctly. 'Now then, onward, if you please.'

The Pan and the Major passed the checkpoint, the guards saluting and raising the barrier without a word. He led The Pan on through the gatehouse, under a portcullis, past a brace of armed guards in flak jackets, over a drawbridge and then through a final checkpoint, also manned, or at least, Grongled, by guards in flak jackets, and into the square. The Major turned to The Pan and addressed him, still in Tithian. His accent was terrible but at least he was making the effort. Either that or it was some form of psychological torture. The Pan tried not to wince.

'I thank you for your patience, Mr Column. If you will accompany me to the Central Police Station, over there,' he waved his free arm at the building in question, across the square. 'I regret that we must report your transgression. You have been found without ID, after all, even if it was at your own front door.'

The Pan could feel himself going white and his hands beginning to shake again. A transfer was better than nothing, but he'd hoped, for a giddy moment, that the Major was going to release him. It appeared not. Arnold's toe jam! So close.

'Is that necessary? Only,' The Pan racked his brains to come up with a decent excuse, 'I think I left the gas on.' Hmm, a bit crap but it would have to do, and at least it was easy to remember.

'I regret so. But in the extenuating circumstances, it's just a formality.'

'You mean, they'll let me go?'

'I'll wager they will.'

'I'll wager.' Not quite as definite as an out-and-out yes, The Pan noticed.

When they arrived at the Central Police Station, a surly desk sergeant looked up at them and, recognising the Major's rank, and possibly, also that he was an intelligence officer, scrambled to his feet. 'Sir,' he saluted.

'I apologise for this intrusion, Sergeant,' said the Major, in a tone of voice that made it clear that he didn't apologise, at all. 'I appreciate you are about to go off duty but Mr Column here has been apprehended without his ID.

'However, he has also locked himself out of his own premises and when apprehended he was trying to get in and retrieve both the ID and his keys. There has been a problem with his record, which I will have my staff rectify this evening. In the meantime, he has promised to present himself here, at zero nine hundred hours tomorrow with his ID.'

The Pan hadn't promised anything but he was in no position to argue. He stood beside the Major, trying not to display any nerves, as the desk sergeant wrote in a notebook. He asked The Pan to spell Frederick, which he did, and it appeared he needed a middle name too, which The Pan gave as Reginald.

'That's all logged, sir,' said the desk sergeant, addressing the Major.

'See you tomorrow morning,' lied The Pan, who had no ID, and certainly wouldn't be presenting himself to the police at any time, let alone the following morning.

The sergeant gave The Pan a contemptuous look, which the Major failed to notice as he led his prisoner outside and removed the handcuff. 'You are free to go now, Mr Column,' he said. Was there something of a twinkle in his eye as he said 'Mr Column'? Possibly, but no matter how great his curiosity, The Pan of Hamgee wasn't going to stop and ask questions.

'Thank you, sir,' he said and bowed. Then he turned on his heel and walked away as briskly as he could without actually running or showing any relief in case the Major took it as evidence of guilt and changed his mind.

What in the name of The Prophet had just happened? It was insane. Nobody came out of the Security HQ. No-one. Ever. The Pan felt dangerously exposed crossing the open corner of the square to the nearest street. This was all very unusual. Was the Grongle Major just toying with him? Was he releasing The Pan, only to shoot him in the back as he walked away? No, no, no, that was no way to think. Anyway, he wouldn't do it here, would he? Not slap bang between the Central Police Station and the Architrave's Palace—or the Security HQ as it was called now. Whatever incredible stroke of luck had caused his deliverance, The Pan knew there was only one thing to do; thank The Prophet for his good fortune and disappear as quickly as possible.

Shaking with excess adrenaline after the fear—and then relief—of his ordeal, he continued to walk briskly across the expanse of cobbles until he reached the nearest street. He cast a brief look back to see the tall form of the Grongle Major heading back to the Security HQ. The Pan turned the corner and walked a hundred yards or so before stopping for a moment to take a few deep breaths and let his shaking subside. It would be foolish to hang around though. He began to walk again; striding out swiftly, putting the Security HQ and that Grongle behind him as fast as he could. As soon as he found a suitable side street, he left the main thoroughfare and broke into a jog. As he distanced himself from their Security HQ there were fewer Grongles, but unfortunately that meant there would be more muggers. The Pan went another couple of blocks on foot, keeping to smaller back streets, just in case there were any members of the security forces about still looking for him. There was a very real chance that Corporal Plympton and his cronies might head out to try and recapture their booty. They might not have put The Pan's extensive criminal record down to dodgy paperwork, even if that weird intelligence officer had.

What happened back there? wondered The Pan.

No point asking. He'd either been drop-dead lucky or someone had helped him out. No. The only person who could conceivably have helped him out was Big Merv, and he didn't know what had happened so it couldn't be him. As far as The Pan was aware, he didn't have any Grongolian contacts either. There was no-one else. The Pan had been drop-dead lucky then. He noticed a couple of shadowy figures behind him and another up ahead. Muggers.

Not quite so drop-dead lucky perhaps, he thought resignedly.

Typical. On a night like this, any decent mugger worth their salt should be down the pub by now, drinking their ill-gotten gains. Unless these two had to divide the takings with a greedy gang boss. Perhaps they did? Whatever it was that had kept them working, The Pan decided to take evasive action early. He turned aside suddenly, grabbed a drainpipe and started to climb. The sound of running feet confirmed their intentions. Better step on it then. The Pan made his way swiftly to the roofs.

The muggers were still cursing and sweating their way after him as he jumped to the roof across the street and ran off along a gully. They'd been too slow to react and now they knew they would never catch up. The sound of their curses drifted up from below as they gave up on him, and returned to ground level.

****

At the Parrot and Screwdriver, The Prophet's Birthday

66

meal that Gladys and Ada were not officially serving was well behind schedule. However, just as the two old ladies were discussing whether they should delay any further, and if they did, whether it was possible to catch up and still close at the legal time by serving two courses at once, the door banged. A cheer rose up from the assembled punters as Trev, who'd popped out, returned. He made his way over to the bar and Gladys took him by the arm and shepherded him off into the Holy of Holies behind the bar.

'How d'it go, son?' asked Gladys once they were closeted away from the prying eyes and ears of the punters in the bar.

'You was right to worry.'

'Yer, I reckoned.'

'I has done what I can.' Trev scratched his head. 'I has called in a few favours.'

Gladys hugged him, 'I just hopes you has sorted it.'

'We'll know soon enough,' said Trev.

'Yer,' Gladys agreed. 'Now,' she brightened, rubbing her hands together, 'I reckons we'd best get started on the soup.'

****

The Pan of Hamgee hid behind a chimney stack, catching his breath and making sure the muggers really hadn't followed him.

He listened.

All was quiet. The city was spread out around him, the lights shining like the peaks of waves on the sea catching the moonlight. His thoughts turned to the coast and home. He missed the sea. He missed his family. He wished … no. Stop. No point making himself miserable. He'd just had the luckiest escape of his life, and he had three boxes of pastries to distribute, and an unofficial Prophet's Birthday celebration to get to. He glanced at his watch. Yeh, one he should have been at over an hour ago. It was difficult to be on time for things and be on the blacklist. The security forces would keep chasing you at the most inopportune times, not to mention those muggers. Still, at least they all appeared to have given up on him for now.

A chill wind blew and The Pan wished he hadn't left his hat and cloak in the snurd, even if he was probably still at large, and alive, because he had. The smart money would be on going to the Parrot on foot over the roofs.

'Stuff that!' said The Pan. He was cold and hungry, and so shaky after his ordeal at the Security HQ that it was probably safer to drive. He'd only slip and fall otherwise, he told himself. Yes, he was being sensible, not lazy at all. He summoned his wheels and waited until they appeared, cruising past with the top down at roof height. He made a running jump and landed untidily in the seat with his feet jammed up against the windscreen. Oh well, you couldn't get it right every time.

Disentangling himself, he took the controls, pressed the button to put up the roof and cranked up the heating. He drove in as pedestrian and legal a manner as he could stand to his destination, stopping only to wipe as much of the foundation as he could off his face and swap his T-shirt with a clean one from the holdall in the boot. He replaced the virulently paisley shirt he'd taken off and sprayed on some deodorant—with more hope than conviction. It was a pity he hadn't time to visit the public baths. After such a protracted bout of cold sweating it would have been a relief for everyone, but there was no time and anyway, The Prophet's Birthday banquet involved some pretty pungent food stuffs. With any luck nobody would notice once they'd served the curried squid. He landed smoothly on Turnadot Street and parked in the alley between the Parrot and its outbuildings.

He climbed out of the snurd and stood surveying his

surroundings. All seemed quiet.

Had they cancelled?

No.

Hmm. Probably best to use the back door though. The main entrance might be locked, even if they were expecting him, because they'd be eating by now. They'd have to be if they wanted to finish the full nine courses of Arnold, The Prophet's Birthday meal and close the pub at anything approaching the legal time.

He retrieved his hat and cloak from the boot and put them on, then grabbed the three boxes of Arnold's Birthday pastries, pressed the self-park button and slipped the snurd keys into his pocket. With a quiet beep of its hooter, the SE2 headed away into the night. Pastries balanced on one arm, The Pan knocked on the door and went in.

****

The Pan hadn't known Ada, Gladys and Their Trev that long but something about them, and the Parrot and Screwdriver, made him feel safe. Perhaps it was just the wonderfully mundane normality of the pub which sat, like an ocean of peaceful calm, at the centre of a life of constant disruption and danger. Perhaps it was the way they, and the punters, accepted him without asking questions. Despite that, he was taken aback when a cheer rose up as he walked in. No, hang on, they'd clocked the three cake boxes he was carrying, that's all. Even so, he couldn't stop the smile that spread across his face. It was good to see them after the experience he'd just had; so, so good. Gladys, Ada and Their Trev had just distributed the crackers. By The Pan's calculation that would mean he'd missed the sweetmeats, the curried squid, the fish pie and the quail. He was sad about the quail and fish pie, and extremely sad about the curried squid—but at least he'd made it in time for the spiced chicken.

'Wotcher lad! Better late than never!' called Trev.

'Yeh,' said The Pan. He was surprised at how shaky his voice sounded. He cleared his throat. 'Happy Prophet's Birthday everyone!' he said, shouting to be heard over the growing whoops and catcalls to add, 'Behold! I bring pastries; Mrs Dingleton's own!'

Another cheer rose up and from across the room. Trev grinned and gave him the thumbs up. Gladys and Ada bustled forward.

'What has you done to your hair?' asked Gladys.

'Where did you get those?' asked Ada.

'Long story,' said The Pan, 'but they're legit, I promise.'

Someone laughed and Gladys swooped on him, swiftly removing the boxes. 'I'll take them pastries before you drops them, young man.'

She seemed to be glowing with pride and gave The Pan a smile of such genuine fondness as she took them that it brought a lump to his throat.

'Don't you want a hand with—' he began but Gladys was already whisking the tower of cake boxes away into the kitchen behind the bar.

Ada took him by the arm.

'You have no idea what a delight it is to see you, young man.'

Right back at you, thought The Pan. But he just smiled.

'Come and sit down.' Ada led him over to where she'd been sitting and patted an empty chair next to hers. 'We're a bit behind. Trev had to pop out and run an errand so we've only eaten the soup and the pie and chips. We're just doing the crackers now.' She held one out to him and when Gladys returned she counted down. 'Ready everyone? One, two, three!'

The sounds of simultaneous bangs from everyone's crackers rang out along with cheering and laughter. The

Pan won his and Ada's, but the gift inside pinged off Norris' head and skittered into Fred 'Fingers' Davies' lap. 'Here!' He lobbed it towards The Pan who had to reach up to catch it as it zipped past his head. 'Nice reactions, son!'

The Pan found himself in proud possession of the tackiest of pink plastic rings. He grinned at Ada, sitting next to him, and raised one eyebrow. 'I'm not sure this goes with my look,' he told her. 'I think you should have it.' He handed it to over.

'Why thank you, young man!' She made a great play of putting it on.

Then Gladys brought the curried squid and a pint appeared beside him from somewhere. 'I has only made one portion of this,' she said as she put the loaded plate in front of him.

The Pan raised his eyebrows in mock surprise, which was difficult because it smelled so good he had to make a concerted effort not to drool at the same time.

'No seconds then?' He flashed her a roguish smile.

'Ner, you cheeky varmint!'

The Pan pulled the plate towards him and the regulars gathered round to watch in fascinated horror as he ate the spicy dish.

Humbert was around somewhere, The Pan presumed, but by some miracle, not in the bar with the punters, or trying to eat his dinner. For the first time since he'd lost his home, his family and any chance of a normal life, The Pan began to feel he belonged somewhere. Here.

He closed his eyes and for a moment, experienced a horrible flashback; the stun shot, the inside of the Security HQ. But then he felt, again, the joyous relief of his unexpected deliverance.

'Are you alright, dear?' Ada was looking at him with a concerned expression.

'Yeh,' The Pan smiled. 'Yeh, I am now.'

'Is you sure? You is looking a bit peaky,' Gladys chipped in.

'I can imagine.'

'Not too spicy is it?' asked Ada.

'No. It's perfect. I'll be alright in a moment. I had a bit of a rough day.'

'Work, dear?'

'Kind of. Let's forget about it.' He put down his knife and fork and raised his glass. 'Cheers everyone!'

Gladys stood up and made the traditional Arnold's Birthday toast. 'Here's to us,' she said.

'The dregs of society!' added Ada with a theatrical wink at The Pan.

'Speak for yourself,' he said in mock offence. The room rang with laughter, everyone drank and all was right with the world.

The end

Other books by M T McGuire

If you'd like to find out what happens next, look out for the next book in this series:

Close Enough
K'Barthan Shorts, Hamgeean Misfit: No 3

As delivery man for Big Merv, one of Ning Dang Po's most powerful crime bosses, The Pan of Hamgee is ordered to deliver a gift to Big Merv's current girlfriend. With a pair of bespoke-made, sapphire and diamond earrings on board, and a trip across the city in the offing, what could possibly go wrong? Everything.

You can also read more about The Pan of Hamgee's adventures in K'Barth in a series of four full-length books.

The K'Barthan Series
All The Pan of Hamgee wants is a quiet life.

So why did he have to fall in love with a woman living a different version of reality, upset a murderous tyrant and then run out of places to hide?

Now all he has to do is face his inner demons, rescue everything he holds dear and save the world, or die trying.

Oh yes, and he's an abject coward.

Great. No pressure then.

Escape From B-Movie Hell
Bronze Medal winner, The Wishing Shelf Book Awards, 2015.

If you asked Andi Turbot whether she had anything in common with Flash Gordon she'd say no, emphatically. Saving the world is for dynamic, go-ahead leaders of men. And while it would be nice to see a woman getting involved for a change, she believes she could be the least well-equipped being in her galaxy for the job.

Then her best friend Eric reveals that he's an extraterrestrial. He's not just any E.T. either. He's Gamalian: seven feet tall, lobster-shaped and covered in marmite-scented goo. Just when Andi's getting used to that he tells her about the apocalypse and really ruins her day.

The human race will perish unless Eric's Gamalian superiors step in. Abducted and trapped on an alien ship, Andi must convince the Gamalians her world is worth saving. Or escape from their clutches and save it herself.

Find out more at: www.hamgee.co.uk/books.html

Author News

Never miss a new release again! Sign up for M T Mail. Just visit this link: http://www.hamgee.co.uk/freebook

You can choose to hear about everything or just new releases. You can also keep up to date with all things M T McGuire by joining her K'Barthan Jolly Japery Facebook Group.

To join, go here: http://bit.ly/JollyJapes

Or you can follow M T McGuire on these social media:

Website: http://www.hamgee.co.uk

Blog: http://www.mtmcguire.co.uk

Twitter: @mtmcguireauthor